Helena Ann's
Storybook Cans

A Steampunk Story

Helena Ann DeLuca

Dorothy-Frances Books

Hi! My name is Vincent Vyner Redsmith. I want to share a steampunk story with you. The story was passed down from my great-great-grandparents. It tells a tale of a time when our steam-powered planet, Zenhollow, was attacked by mechanical biting beetles. It's a tale of a distinguished queen who ruled a long, long time ago, Queen Henrietta Cogwright. She saved the planet and all the mechanical animals that lived at that time. The queen's robot, Stannum Wolfram Metallum, will unlock the story, so let's follow him. I never get tired of the riveted rhymes!

The author wishes to thank the creator of the steampunk character, Vincent: Dorota@dorotkazoz12/Etsy.

Helena Ann's Storybook Cans
A Steampunk Story

Published byDorothy-Frances Books®
First Edition; First Printing
www.dfbooks.com

ISBN-13: 978-1-7334865-3-8

Walk with me as I unlock this door, and you'll
see things you've never seen before. Our beautiful
queen, who rules the planet Zenhollow, has asked
me to greet you, so if you would kindly follow.

Queen Cogwright arrived in her airship quite disturbed because of an awful rumor she'd heard. And for this type of rumor, the queen had no sense of humor!

When they told the queen the rumors she'd heard were all true, the gears in her head steamed up—what should she do?

Mechanical beetles had made entry through a portal from space—an open door. It was an assault the beetles from Scaratunia had never done before.

They entered a portal door that was left open by mistake and seized the moment to make mischief and cause harm and heartache.

These beetles from Scaratunia were attacking all of the planet's steampunk animals. The beetles were flying around, biting the animals with their mechanical mandibles. Zenhollow had been quiet since being founded, but now the biting beetles had them surrounded.

The queen called on her locomotives, tractors, and air-shooters, too. She knew she had to act quickly, though, with no further ado.

The queen had two daughters, princesses, who were both stylish and smart. They could see that something was tearing their queen mother apart.

One princess took out her lucky-punky
heart and put on her funky thinking hat,
the one she always used to solve things,
along with help from mother's cat.

The queen's royal cat had a perrrrfect way
to deal with these nasty little bugs—they'd
use all their gears and bolts to get rid of the
mechanical little thugs!

The queen's very intellectual eagle agreed with the princess and the royal cat. There wasn't anything else that could come close to working any better than that. Yes! Gears and bolts—bolts and gears—that's the beetles' biggest fears.

Together they finalized their thoughts and ideas and came up with a plan—they would shoot the gears and bolts at the beetles using the queen's steam-engine clan.

Everyone worked to get the locomotives ready at the steaming-up station. Engines filled up with lots of gears and bolts and prepared to line up in formation.

Bird flew over one of the sites on the north side to see how things were going . . . the size of the defense was impressive, and it was growing and growing!

Octopus had to admit that he was glad he
lived under the sea at times like this—but
helped by using his eight arms to fling gears
to the surface, so he'd not be remiss.

Seahorse swept up the gears and bolts lying around on the ocean floor. She tossed them up one by one until finally there were no more.

Lance the locomotive threw his gears and bolts way up high. One of the bolts even hit a beetle square in the eye!

Emma revved her engine and let her gears fly high into the sky. And, she hit several nasty-acting beetles on her very first try!

The head beetle, a bragging brute of a bug, knew he was losing and was no longer so smug.

That nasty old head beetle once hit, ran away and retreated. He told the others to run, too, realizing they were defeated!

Mouse, who lived on the south side of
Zenhollow, felt sad—many of his friends
up north had been bitten pretty bad.

Rabbit was overwhelmed—those beetles gave her quite a challenging chase! She was glad to be back to normal, with all her gears stored back in place.

Then there was Giraffe, who because she's so tall, got hit in the head many times— twenty in all!

And Tiger, she felt thrilled the beetles were no longer around—there were so many gears and bolts all over the ground.

Parrot was seriously over it, to be honest, and he felt the whole assault was surely the oddest!

Kangaroo had hopped to and fro to avoid getting bitten, seeing all the gears and bolts flying around—she found herself smitten.

Bear was so glad that all the beetles were gone. The battle had gone on from dusk until dawn. The plan to use the steam engines' gears and bolts had proved successful, even though for many hours, it was extremely stressful!

Lion was thankful for the peaceful aftermath, having been a victim of the beetles' nasty biting wrath. And Lion, who is quite vain, was not happy losing a piece of his mane. Giraffe and Tiger cleaned up with their sisters and brothers. Lion and Bear helped Kangaroo, Rabbit, and the others.

All the gears and bolts were soon cleaned up and put away, and they all gave three cheers to Zenhollow. Hip hip hooray!

I'll be locking the door of this story for now, in Zenhollow, where we all dwell. The robot, the queen and princesses, and we steampunk animals all wish you well!

Can you help Vincent find
these 15 items in the book?
Each item can be found
within one of the images
of the story. Good luck!

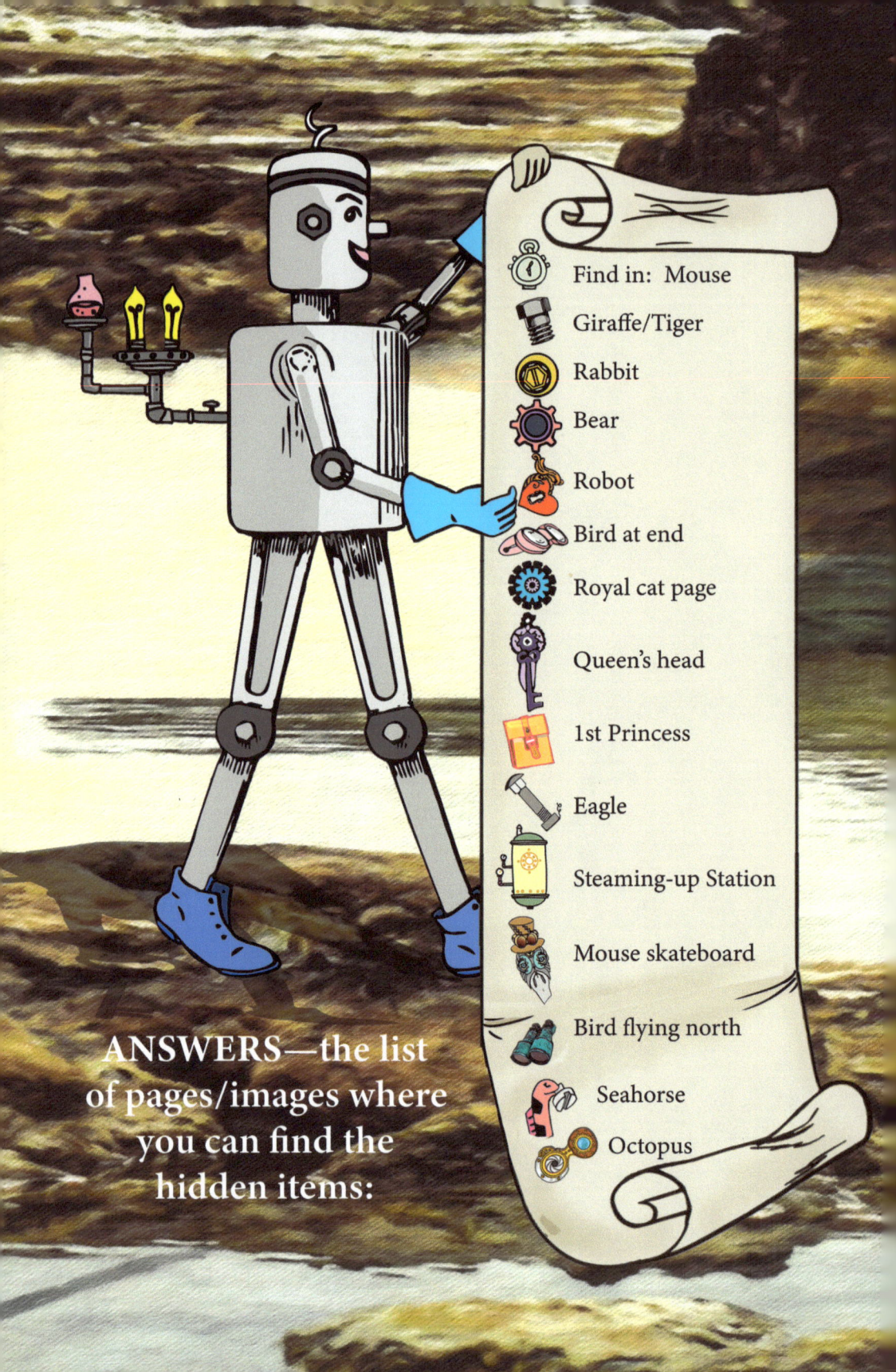

Find in: Mouse

Giraffe/Tiger

Rabbit

Bear

Robot

Bird at end

Royal cat page

Queen's head

1st Princess

Eagle

Steaming-up Station

Mouse skateboard

Bird flying north

Seahorse

Octopus

ANSWERS—the list
of pages/images where
you can find the
hidden items:

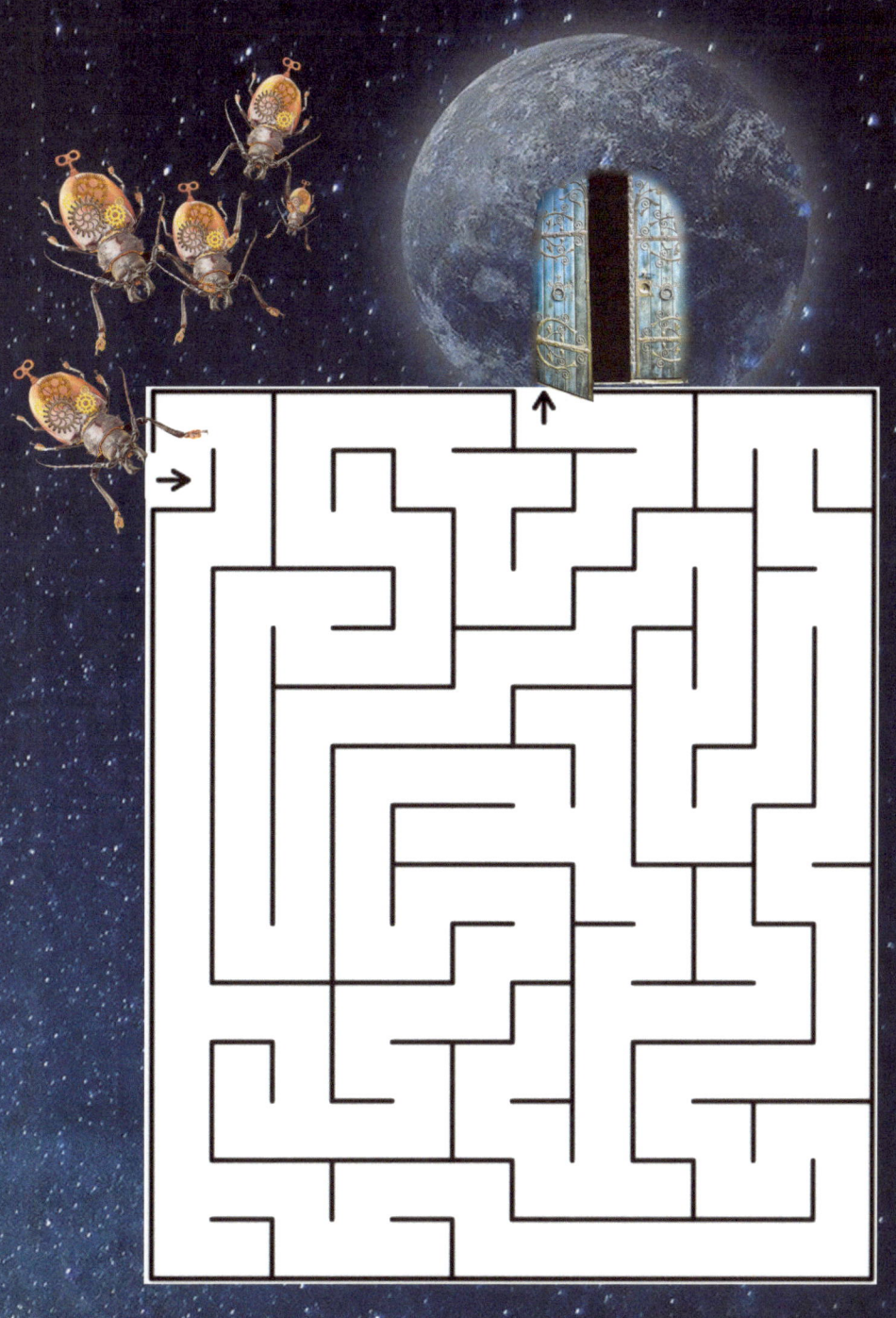

Trace the path the beetles took to reach
the open door on Zenhollow.

Maze solution: